HOW TO PRAY

Beginners Guide

Muhammad Salih

TABLE OF CONTENT

What invalidates Solat

Conclusion

Reference

INTRODUCTION

The first act of worship in Islam that was required was salah, and there were no other forms of worship at the time. Three years prior to the Hijra, it became mandatory in Makkah. If all worship was required on earth, then Allah had invited the Prophet (pbuh) to perform salah in the sky. It is also referred to as Mi'raj. This night, the Prophet traveled with Jibril (May Allah be pleased with him) to the heavens, where they saw many wonders and attained a height that not even his traveler could.

During that conversation, the Prophet received Salah as a unique gift for himself and his community. Allah did not want prayer to be required on earth, the wellspring of dirt and desire, therefore He invited the Prophet there. The fact that prayer is the first act of devotion and that it must be directed toward the skies are two of its greatest qualities. The manifestation of this happiness is Mi'raj Day.

On the day after the Night Journey, the Prophet commenced the required prayer. The Zuhr prayer, led by the angel Jibreel (May Allah be pleased with him), was the first required Salat that the Prophet recited. The Zuhr prayer is therefore referred to as the first prayer.

The Prophet Muhammad (pbuh) did not offer his first prayer at dawn, as should be observed. This is due to the requirement that a description of how to execute prayer be made in order for prayer to be assumed and assigned. The dawn prayer did not accomplish this, hence it was not necessary for the worship leader to offer it prior to the declaration. When anything is said, it must be done immediately after; this is what happened during the noon prayer when Jibreel (May Allah be pleased with him) taught the Prophet about it.

CHAPTER 1

Solat for Beginners:
A Step-by-Step Guide to Islamic Prayer

The spiritual bond between a servant and our Lord is bolstered by the lovely act of worship known as solat. It is an act of submission to Allah SWT in which the believer places their whole and unwavering confidence in Him SWT.

Allah (swt) declares in the Qur'an:

إِنَّنِىٓ أَنَا ٱللَّهُ لَآ إِلَٰهَ إِلَّآ أَنَا۠ فَٱعۡبُدۡنِى وَأَقِمِ ٱلصَّلَوٰةَ لِذِكۡرِىٓ

There is no other god save me, so worship me and offer prayers to remember me, insha'Allah.

Suratu Taha (14 vs 14)

It was Allah s.w.t. who reminded Prophet Musa a.s. Knowing, loving, and eventually worshiping our Lord is the reason we were created. Through prayer, we can connect with and remember Allah s.w.t., our Creator. To devote ourselves to responding to our Master's call, we disengage from worldly distractions.

As it did for Prophet Muhammad s.a.w. during difficult times, such remembrance can bring peace, solace, and comfort to a troubled heart.

Additionally, solat is a spiritual act of worship as well as a physical one, allowing the believer to interact and be closest to Allah s.w.t. Language-wise, solat is equivalent to dua (pure prayer), which establishes a direct line between the servant and the Lord. It is seen as the believer's ascension (mi'raj), a time when we can transcend the human realm and establish a connection with God.

In the context of fiqh, the term "solat" refers to a predetermined series of gestures and vocalizations that begin with the takbir and culminate with the salam. These particular recitations and deeds are an essential part of this act of worship and must be carried out with the appropriate reverence.

We shall look at the importance of solat in Islam as well as its advantages, requirements, and how to execute it in this post. We'll also go over the things that could disrupt solat and offer some duas that you could say once the prayer is over.

CHAPTER 2

Why Solat is important

In Islam, solat is of utmost importance. Solat is the essential pillar on which the entire religion rests, as the Prophet Muhammad s.a.w. emphasized in a hadith: that the fundamental tenet of the entire religion is solat:

الصَّلاةُ عِمادُ الدِّينِ

The foundational principle of this religion is solat.

(Shub Al-Iman)

Solat is so important that during the Prophet Muhammad s.a.w.'s miraculous voyage to Isra' Mi'raj, it was revealed to him directly. At Sidratul Muntaha (the lote tree at the farthest reach), a distance that not even the Angel Jibril could cross, Allah s.t. gave him this important piece of legislation.

There is significance to the solat gift. It is a strategy for obtaining success in this life and the next. According to the Quran, Allah s.w.t. considers those believers successful who humble themselves in prayer:

قَدْ أَفْلَحَ ٱلْمُؤْمِنُونَ. ٱلَّذِينَ هُمْ فِى صَلَاتِهِمْ خَاشِعُونَ

Christians who are humble in prayer are successful in their faith.

(Qur'an Al-Mu'minin, 23:1-2)

In times of adversity and sadness, Prophet Muhammad s.a.w. found comfort in prayer. In order to move forward in life, he would first perform wudhu (ablution), after which he would build his prayer:

أَنَّ الرَّسُولَ صَلَّى اللهُ عَلَيهِ وَسَلَّمَ كَانَ إِذَا حَزَبَهُ أمرٌ فَزِعَ إِلَى الصَّلَاةِ

Rasulullah s.a.w. would engage in prayer (solat) whenever something upset him.

in Sunan Abi Daud

The Prophet s.a.w. liked conducting his prayers despite having his share of sad circumstances, as though solat had caused joy to bloom in his heart. It is reported in a hadith that the Prophet Muhammad, s.a.w., said:

وَجُعِلَ قُرَّةُ عَيْنِي فِي الصَّلَاةِ

And prayer is the joy of my eyes.

Sunan An-Nasi

For Muslims, prayer serves as a source of spiritual and emotional nutrition rather than just a ritualistic activity. It gives the servant a way to contact Allah (swt) in order to ask for His direction and unendig mercy. As a result, it is extremely valuable to believers and acts as a constant reminder of our faith and purpose in life.

We should take use of the chance during each prayer to express our hopes and fears to Allah s.w.t., especially while in the position of prostration, whether we feel fear, worry, or anxiety owing to financial, work-related, or any other issues. According to a hadith reported by Imam Muslim, the Prophet (s.a.w.) said:

أَقْرَبُ ما يَكونُ العَبْدُ مِن رَبِّهِ، وهو ساجِدٌ، فأَكْثِرُوا الدُّعاءَ

When a servant is prostrating (in sujud), he is closest to his Lord, so you should intensify your prayers at that time.

Muslim tradition (Sahih)
By fostering a sense of community among us, group prayers might further improve this experience.

CHAPTER 3

Advantages of Solat

For people who frequently practice solat, there are a variety of advantages.

1. Solat cleanses us of our transgressions

First, as stated in a hadith that compares solat to the purifying power of a flowing river, solat purifies us from our sins.

مَثَلُ الصَّلَوَاتِ الخَمْسِ كَمَثَلِ نَهْرٍ جَارٍ، غَمْرٍ علَى بَابِ أَحَدِكُمْ، يَغْتَسِلُ منه كُلَّ يَومٍ خَمْسَ مَرَّاتٍ

The five (obligatory) solat are compared to a river that flows past one of your doors and into which he bathes five times per day.

[Sahih Muslim]

2. Solat guards against immorality and evil.

In the Quran, Allah s.t. says:

إِنَّ ٱلصَّلَوٰةَ تَنْهَىٰ عَنِ ٱلْفَحْشَآءِ وَٱلْمُنكَرِ ۗ وَلَذِكْرُ ٱللَّهِ أَكْبَرُ ۗ وَٱللَّهُ يَعْلَمُ مَا تَصْنَعُونَ

Prayer does, in fact, dissuade one from immorality and wickedness.

(Ankabut Al-Surah 45:51)

3. Those who observe Solat are illuminated by it.
The unique impacts of solat will also be felt in the Hereafter.
When we assemble on the day of the resurrection, there will be
light that is illuminated on a solat observer, enabling that person
to stand out among the rest of humanity.

من حافَظَ عليها كانت لَه نورًا وبُرهانًا ونجاةً إلى يومِ القيامةِ

The day of the resurrection will provide illumination, direction, and
salvation to everybody who observes it (solat).

Muhsin Ahmad

4. Solat strengthens psychological and spiritual stability
Solat strengthens mental and spiritual stability, too. The Quran
describes those who perform solat on a regular basis as being
steadfast and able to withstand both good and terrible times. In
the Qur'an, Allah (swt) declares:

إِنَّ ٱلْإِنسَـٰنَ خُلِقَ هَلُوعًا. إِذَا مَسَّهُ ٱلشَّرُّ جَزُوعًا. وَإِذَا مَسَّهُ ٱلْخَيْرُ مَنُوعًا. إِلَّا ٱلْمُصَلِّينَ. ٱلَّذِينَ هُمْ
عَلَىٰ صَلَاتِهِمْ دَائِمُونَ

In fact, anxiousness was present when humankind was created.
Except for those who are dedicated to prayer, he becomes
anxious when anything evil touches him and withholds when
something wonderful does, except for those who are committed to
prayer and who pray without ceasing

Al-Ma'arij, verses 70:19–23

The first line of the verse claims that "humans were created in a state of anxiety," alluding to our intrinsic propensity to worry about our existence, our future, and other aspects of life. The next section discusses how people respond to the various events we encounter in life. We feel nervous and worried when we come upon wickedness or suffering. We worry that excellent things will be taken away from us when we receive them.

The text does, however, note that there are persons who are devoted to prayer who are exceptions to this typical behavior. These people never stop praying, asking Allah for assistance and guidance in every circumstance.

Through prayer, we are able to communicate with Allah (swt) and ask for His assistance and direction in all spheres of life, including emotional regulation, stress management, and navigating challenging circumstances.

CHAPTER 4

The Requirements of Solat

The following are considered prerequisites for solat by the Syafi'i school of thinking in (mazhab):

1. The solat time arrives. The position of the sun determines the time for each prayer, and it is imperative that the prayer be offered at the appointed moment.

Muslims are obligated to conduct wudhu (ablution) prior to solat.

2. Wudhu (ablution): Before solat, Muslims must do wudhu. In wudhu, specific body parts, such as the hands, face, arms, and feet, are washed in a particular way.

3. Ghusl: Ghusl is a full-body purification that must be performed after specific occurrences including sex, menstruation, and postpartum bleeding. Before performing solat, a person must perform ghusl if they are significantly impure.

4. Wearing an aurat entails covering the complete body, with the exception of the face and hands, for both men and women. For men, this implies the region between the navel and the knees.

Continue the solat and cover any exposed portions of the aurat if necessary while the prayer is being said. Immediately after noticing it, close it. Your solat could be broken if that happens.

5. Cleanliness of the body, the attire, and the site of solat: Make sure that your body, your attire, and the area where you will be praying are all clean and impure-free.

6. Muslims must perform solat while facing the Kaaba in Makkah, which is the direction of the qiblah.

CHAPTER 5

Performing the Solat

The process of solat entails surrendering your complete being to Allah s.w.t. through vocal utterances (qauli), bodily gestures (fi'li), and a focused mind and heart (qalbiy).

Here is a step-by-step explanation of how to perform solat, as per mazhab Syafi'i:

1. Establish intention

Creating the intention (niyyah) in our hearts is the first step in performing our solat, just like it is with all other acts of worship. This essentially defines the kind of solat that we want to carry out.

Although it is sunnah and not wajib (obligatory) to verbally express our intention, doing so can help us to focus on our solat and reaffirm our intention.

For instance, if you want to offer a private subuh prayer, you can say:

أُصَلِّي فَرضَ صَلَاةَ الصُّبحِ رَكعَتَينِ لِلَّهِ تَعَالَى

I'm going to perform the required subuh prayer in two raka'at for Allah (swt).

When we pray in congregation, we must state whether we are praying on behalf of the imam (the person who leads the prayer) or a ma'mum (follower or member of the congregation).

The Imam should:

أُصَلِّي فَرضَ صَلَاةَ الصُّبحِ رَكعَتَينِ إِمَامًا لِلَّهِ تَعَالَى

I'm going to do the required subuh prayer in the role of an imam for two raka'at.

We must designate our goal when we pray in congregation as either the imam (the person who conducts the congregational prayer) or Ma'amuum (follower or adherent).

to the Imam

أُصَلِّي فَرضَ صَلَاةَ الصُّبحِ رَكعَتَينِ إِمَامًا لِلَّهِ تَعَالَى

As the Imam, I will offer the two-raka'at subuh prayer as required for Allah (swt).

For the Ma'amuum

أُصَلِّي فَرضَ صَلَاةَ الصُّبحِ رَكعَتَينِ مَأُمُومًا لِلَّهِ تَعَالَى

As Ma'mum, I'll offer the two-raka'at compulsory subuh prayer to Allah ta'ala.

Being present (hudhur) in both the heart and mind is crucial during solat. In order to do this, we must be mindful of both our actions and our prayerful speech. Despite the possibility of distractions, we ought to make an effort to concentrate during our prayers.

Actually, taking wudhu—a mindful cleansing of every part of the body in preparation for submission to prayer—is the first step in preparing for a mindful solat.

2. Takbiratul Ihram

The first step in entering the state of prayer is takbiratul Ihram. To do this, raise both hands so that the palms are parallel to the floor and the thumbs are positioned at the level of the shoulders.

Say the takbir "Allahu Akbar" to signal the start of the prayer. Even if it's just a whisper, it's important to say the takbir loud enough for you to hear your own voice.

It is important to note that a takbir that is just spoken silently in the heart does not satisfy this criteria.

3. If you can, stand.

Standing is an essential (rukun) component of solat during fardhu (obligatory) prayers. While standing, cross your right hand over your left, placing your hands anywhere below your chest and above your navel.

While adhering to these rules is important, remember that Allah (swt) is Most Compassionate and Most Merciful. If someone is unable to stand for a justifiable reason, such as illness or injury, they may sit in its place. Because of this, it's possible to see some elderly people participating in the congregational prayers while seated in the mosque.

Let's keep doing all we can to fulfill our religious commitments while being aware of our bodily constraints.

It is sunnah to recite the first dua, Dua Iftitah, while standing and right after the takbir.

اللّٰهُ أَكْبَرُ كَبِيرًا وَالْحَمْدُ لِلّٰهِ كَثِيْرًا وَسُبْحَانَ اللّٰهِ بُكْرَةً وَأَصِيْلًا .وَجَّهْتُ وَجْهِيَ لِلَّذِيْ فَطَرَ السَّمَاوَاتِ وَالْأَرْضَ حَنِيْفًا مُسْلِمًا وَمَا أَنَا مِنَ الْمُشْرِكِيْنَ . إِنَّ صَلَاتِيْ وَنُسُكِيْ وَمَحْيَايَ وَمَمَاتِيْ لِلّٰهِ رَبِّ الْعَالَمِيْنَ لَا شَرِيْكَ لَهُ وَبِذَلِكَ أُمِرْتُ وَأَنَا مِنَ الْمُسْلِمِيْنَ

All hail Kabir, Akbar!

Thank you, Kathryn.

Subhanallah, Bukratan, wa a'l

Wajjahtu Fatras-Samwti wal-Ardh Wajhiya lillazi

Hanfan Musliman Wa-m ana Muslimek

Inna "alt," Wa-nusuk," Wa-mahya," Wamamt Lilli Rabbil "Lamn"

L'syarka la Hu wa bizlika umirtu wa ana minal muslimn

Almighty and Greatest Allah

All honor and glory to Him.

Each and every moment, Allah The Most Exalted

I'm in front of the person who made the earth and the sky.

I humbly bow to Allah, and I most definitely do not belong to the group who equates Allah with other entities.

My supplication, good acts, life, and death are all for Allah, the Creator of the universes.

I have been instructed to act in this manner, and I am a follower of Islam. He has neither a partner nor a parallel in any way.

Only the first raka'at of prayer is reserved for the recitation of dua iftitah.

4. Say Surat Al-Fatiha.

It is sunnah to recite the ta'awwuz silently before reciting Surah Al-Fatiha:

أَعُوذُ بِاللهِ مِنَ الشَّيْطَانِ الرَّجِيمِ

Rojim A'uzubillahi Minasshaitonir

I turn to Allah for protection from the evil Syaitan.

After that, say Surah Al-Fatiha. Please be aware that reading
Surah Al-Fatihah silently in your heart does not constitute as
spoken recitation. Like the takbir, you must say it aloud, even if it
is whispered.

الرَّحمٰنِ الرَّحيمِ. مالِكِ يَومِ الدّينِ

إِيّاكَ نَعبُدُ وَإِيّاكَ نَستَعينُ

اهدِنَا الصِّراطَ المُستَقيمَ

صِراطَ الَّذِينَ أَنعَمتَ عَلَيهِم غَيرِ المَغضُوبِ عَلَيهِم وَلَا الضّالّينَ

———

Bismillāhir-Raḥmānir-Raḥīm.

Assalamu alaykum wa rabbi lamin.

Ar-Raḥmānir-Raḥīm.

Mliki Yawmid.

Iyyka nabudu wa Iyyka nastan.

Ihdināṣ-ṣirāṭal-mustaqīm.

"Irallazna anamta ghayril-maghbi alayhim wa-llln"

———

In the name of the Most Merciful and Compassionate God.

Praise be to Allah, the creator of all things.

The Kind and the Merciful. On the Day of Reckoning, the ruler.

We worship you alone, and we only turn to you for assistance.

Please lead us in a straight line.

those whom You have placed Your Grace upon,
not those with whom You are angry or who have gone astray.

Amiin.

———

It is sunnah to recite the following prayers out loud: Subuh and Friday prayers, the first two raka'at of Maghrib and Isyak, the two sunnah eid prayers (solat sunnah aidilfitri and aidiladha), istisqa' prayer (solat to seek rain), khusuf prayer (moon eclipse), terawih prayers, and witr prayers in Ramadan.

Study Surah Al-Fatiha: Its Purpose and Benefits.

When there are no muhrim men around—guys she is not allowed to have intimate or physical contact with since they are not related to her by blood or marriage—women are also authorized to recite aloud.

It is crucial to understand how to recite Surah Al-Fatihah since it is a crucial component of the solat.
But don't worry if you're still learning; just do your best to recite it. To aid with your recitation during prayer, you might even bring a piece of paper. It is advised to select an imam who can recite more fluently for congregational prayer.

Watch: Beginner's Guide to Learning the Qur'an

It is advised to recite any memorized surah of your choice as an added sunnah after reciting Surah Al-Fatihah. For instance, you might recite Surah Al-Ikhlas or Ayatul Kursi following Surah Al-Fatihah.

It is advised to pick a surah for the second raka'at that does not follow the first surah in the Quran's order.

Observation: It is sunnah to recite Surah Al-Fatihah in the first two raka'at of solat, and then only one additional surah.

5. Complete ruku.

Raise your hands and chant "Allahu Akbar" as you move into the ruku' stance. The phrase "transition from one movement to another" refers to this change in direction and is known as the "takbiratul intiqal."

As you approach the ruku' position, slowly bring your hands to your knees.

Three times the dua ruku'

سُبْحَانَ رَبِّيَ العَظِيمِ وَبِحَمْدِهِ

'Azeem wa bihamdihi Subhana Robbiyal

Praise and honor be to my Almighty Lord.

After the dua, pause for a very short period of time (tuma'ninah) so that your movements are not hurried, and then proceed to the next stage. Applying this break is necessary also in each subsequent stage.

6. Tidal

Raise your hands, and while saying the following, get back to standing.

سَمِعَ اللهُ لِمَنْ حَمِدَهُ

Sami'Allahu liman Hamida

The praisers of Allah are heard.

beginner's guide to female jihad prayer

Put your hands at your sides while lowering them gradually. Raise your hands and say the following aloud while standing straight up:

رَبَّنَا وَلَكَ الْحَمْدُ

Rababna wala Kal-Hamd

All praises go to You, O Lord.

7. Sujud

As you bow (sujud), recite the takbir. Prior to placing your hands or forehead down, place your knee first. You should have a clean forehead. Any portion of your forehead that is covered by your songkok, tudung, or hair should be visible.

Recite the following three times while in the sujud position:

سُبْحَانَ رَبِّيَ الأَعْلَى وَبِحَمْدِهِ

I am Subhana Robbiyal A'laa Wa Bihamdihi.

Salutations to my Lord, the Most High.

8. Take a seat between two sujud (julus)

After the sujud, assume the julus (seated) position while reciting "Allahu Akbar." It is sunnah to sit in the iftirash position, resting on your left foot and leaning on your raised right leg. Your right toes should all point in the direction of prayer.

How to perform Julus Sit in Solat, a step-by-step guide for Muslims

Your hands are on your lap, resting on the tops of your knees.

But for some people, like those who might have an injury, this position can be difficult. In that case, you should feel comfortable sitting up straight.

Read the dua once you are seated properly:

رَبِّ اغْفِرْ لِي، وَارْحَمْنِي، وَاجْبُرْنِي، وَارْفَعْنِي، وَارْزُقْنِي، وَاهْدِنِي، وَعَافِنِي، وَاعْفُ عَنِّي

Robbighfirli warhamni warfa'ni warzuqni wahdini wa 'aafini wa'fu 'anni

O my Lord, pardon me; have mercy on me; bolster me; elevate my station; support me; direct me; grant me well-being.

9. Sujud once more

Saying "Allahu Akbar" while returning to the sujud stance.

Sujud prayer in Islam: a step-by-step guide

Recite these three verses while bowing down:

سُبْحَانَ رَبِّيَ الأَعْلَى وَبِحَمْدِهِ

A'laa wa bihamdihi Subhana robbiyal

Glory to my Lord, the Highest

Alhamdulillah, upon fulfilling the second sujud, you have now finished one raka'at of solat.

Start the subsequent raka'at slowly. Start the next raka'at by rising to your feet once more. Follow steps 3 through 9 to finish the following raka'at.

To perform the tasyahhud awwal whilst in the second raka'at, sit down after the second sujud:

اَلتَّحِيَّاتُ الْمُبَارَكَاتُ الصَّلَوَاتُ الطَّيِّبَاتُ لِلهِ
اَلسَّلاَمُ عَلَيْكَ أَيُّهَا النَّبِيُّ وَرَحْمَةُ اللهِ وَبَرَكَاتُهُ

السَّلاَمُ عَلَيْنَا وَعَلَى عِبَادِ اللهِ الصَّالِحِينَ أَشْهَدُ أَنْ لاَ إِلَهَ إِلاَّ اللهُ وَ أَشْهَدُ أَنَّ مُحَمَّدًا رَسُولُ اللهِ اَللَّهُمَّ صَلِّ عَلَى سَيِدِنَا مُحَمَّدٍ وعلى آل سيدنا محمد

Attahiyatul-mubaarakaatus solawatut toyyibaatu lillah
Assalaamu 'alaikum wa 'alaa 'ibadillahi wa barakaatuhu
Assalaamu 'alaina wa 'alaa 'ibadillahi-solihiin
Ashadu anla ilaha illAllah, and ashadu anna muhammadar
rasulullah Allahumma solli 'ala sayyidina Muhammad wa ali
sayyidina Muhammad

Greetings, prayers, and salutations of good acts to Allah. God's
kindness and His blessings be upon you, O Prophet, and peace.
God's slaves who do well will be blessed with peace, including us.
I vouch for Muhammad as God's representative and messenger,
and I vouch for there being no other deity than Him.
In the name of Allah, give blessings to Muhammad and his family.

After that, stand up slowly. After completing the tasyahhud awwal,
it is sunnah to raise your hands as you enter the third raka'at.

10. Take up the final tahiyyat seat.

Sit in the tawarruk position for the final raka'at. The term "tahiyyat
akhir" refers to the sitting position in which you are on your hips,
particularly your left backside. Your left leg is tucked under your
right leg as your right foot is raised.

Tahiyyat akhir: A step-by-step guide to Islamic prayer

After settling into a comfortable sitting position, say the following dua:

اَلتَّحِيَّاتُ الْمُبَارَكَاتُ الصَّلَوَاتُ الطَّيِّبَاتُ لِلَّهِ

اَلسَّلاَمُ عَلَيْكَ أَيُّهَا النَّبِيُّ وَرَحْمَةُ اللهِ وَبَرَكَاتُهُ

السَّلاَمُ عَلَيْنَا وَعَلَى عِبَادِ اللهِ الصَّالِحِينَ أَشْهَدُ أَنْ لاَ إِلَهَ إِلاَّ اللهُ وَأَشْهَدُ أَنَّ مُحَمَّدًا رَسُولُ اللهِ

In the name of Allah, Attahiyyatul Mubaarakaatus Solawatut Toyyibaatu
Assalamu alaykum warahmatullahi wabarakatuh,
Assalamu'alaikum wa 'ala 'ibadillahi wa ashhadu ann la ilaha illahi wa ashhadu anna muhammadar-rasulullah

Salutations, prayers, and good acts to Allah in blessing. O Prophet, and Attahiyyatul mubaarakaatus solawatut toyyibaatu lillah, may peace be upon you.
Assalamu alaykum warahmatullahi wabarakatuh,
Assalamu'alaikum wa 'ala 'ibadillahi wa ashhadu ann la ilaha illahi wa ashhadu anna muhammadar-rasulullah

Salutations, prayers, and good acts to Allah in blessing. O Prophet, may Allah's mercy and His blessings be upon you. May God's blessings be upon us and his faithful servants. Muhammad is God's servant and His messenger, and I attest that there is no other god except He.

When you get to "Ashhadu a la ilaha illAllah," emphasize "..illAllah" (but God) by lifting your right index finger while clenching your other right fingers.

11. Prayer (Salawat) upon the noble Prophet Muhammad (S.A.W).

Proceed to Selawat Ibrahimiyyah

اَللّٰهُمَّ صَلِّ عَلَى سَيِّدِنَا مُحَمَّدٍ وَعَلَى آلِ سَيِّدِنَا مُحَمَّدٍ كَمَا صَلَّيْتَ عَلَى سَيِّدِنَا إِبْرَاهِيمَ وَعَلَى آلِ سَيِّدِنَا إِبْرَاهِيمَ وَبَارِكْ عَلَى سَيِّدِنَا مُحَمَّدٍ وَعَلَى آلِ سَيِّدِنَا مُحَمَّدٍ كَمَا بَارَكْتَ عَلَى سَيِّدِنَا إِبْرَاهِيمَ وَعَلَى آلِ سَيِّدِنَا إِبْرَاهِيمَ فِي العَالَمِينَ إِنَّكَ حَمِيدٌ مَجِيدٌ

Allahumma solli 'ala sayyidina Muhammad wa 'ala ali sayyidina Muhammad Kama sollaita 'ala sayyidina ibrahim Wa 'ala sayyidina ibrahim Wabarik 'ala sayyidina Muhammad wa 'ala ali sayyidina Muhammad Kama barakta 'ala sayyidina ibrahim Fil 'alamina innaka hamidun-majiid.

Please, Allah, extend Your mercy to Muhammad and his family in the same way that you did to Ibrahim and his clan.
Allah, please bless Muhammad and his family, just as You did for Ibrahim and his.

Because You Truly Deserve Praise and Are Glorious.

12. Say Salaam

You finish the solat by first looking over your right shoulder and saying:

السَّلَامُ عَلَيْكُم وَرَحمَةُ اللهِ

Salutations and Allah's peace to you

I wish you blessings and peace.

Then, turn your head over your left shoulder and say these words again.

Islam prayer: A step-by-step guide

13. Tertib

Tertib in solat refers to doing the prayer's listed steps in the right order and following the proper sequence.

The prayer may become invalid if any of these postures or gestures are made out of sequence, in which case we would have to recite the entire prayer from scratch.

As a result, it's crucial to understand and adhere to the correct tertib in solat.

How many solats are in a single raka'at?

There are five fardhu prayers performed each day, each with a different quantity of raka'at:

Subuh, 2 rakats; Zohor, 4 rakats; Asar, 4 rakats; Maghrib, 3 rakats; Ishai, 4 rakats.

Please follow steps 1 through 9 for the first raka'at of the two-raka'at Subuh prayer, then steps 3 through 12 for the second raka'at.

Do steps 1 through 9 in the first raka'at if you are praying for Zohor, Asar, or Ishai, and then steps 3 through 9 in the second raka'at. After finishing the second raka'at, don't forget to do the first tasyahhud. Repeat steps 3 through 9 for the third raka'at after that. The fourth raka'at should be performed in the same manner, up to step 12.

CHAPTER 6

Are there any variations in the Solat movements between men and women?

According to the Syafi'i mazhab, there are only two minor changes between the movements of solat for men and women. The variations are discernible at two positions:[1]

1. Men are instructed to spread their arms wide while holding their knees during ruku, whereas women are instructed to tighten their arms and bring them somewhat closer together.

2. Men should spread their arms wider and leave a bit wider space between their hips and stomach during sujud. Women, on the other hand, should maintain a close hip and stomach position and keep their arms slightly closer together.

CHAPTER 7

What invalidates or destroys the solat?

1. Talking, laughing, or using any other vocal expressions that are unrelated knowingly.

2. Consuming food or beverages

3. Making any three consecutive movements that are unrelated to the action at hand, such as gesturing or walking. These are significant limb motions, not small ones like the fluttering of our fingers or the closing of our eyes.

It is important to note that the Syafi'i school holds that actions that are out of our control, such sneezing or shaking, do not interrupt the prayer.

Would it be a solat violation if someone forgot the raka'at they were in?
No, that's the answer. He would have to decide on the number of raka'at, typically the lower raka'at, that he feels most confident (yaqeen) with. He should conduct sujud sahwi at the conclusion of the solat and right before extending the salam.

Sujud Sahwi is carried out to make up for a lapse or error in their prayer. In the Syafi'i school of thinking, it is also sunnah for someone to perform sujud sahwi if they forget or have questions about completing certain requirements in prayer, such as:

1. The very first Tasyahud

2. The dua qurban (subuh prayer)

3. Reciting the Shahadah for the Prophet Muhammad s.a.w.

Step 11 (Selawat Ibrahimiyyah), the final raka'at, should be completed without saying the salam first. Instead, bow down and say the dua three times while doing so:

سُبْحَانَ مَنْ لَا يَنَامُ وَلَا يَسْهُو

Yas-hu Subhaana man la yanaam wa

Glory to the One who never forgets or slumbers

The julus (sitting) position should be adopted after the sujud (prostration).

Islamic prayer: Julus sit in solat, step-by-step

While reciting the dua three times, perform a second sujud.

After finishing the prayer, return to the julus stance and say salam to the right and left without reciting any further dua.

You must perform sujud sahwi during the imam's prostration if you are following him during solat.

After solat, what duas can we read?

You have a special chance to connect with Allah SWT after your solat and ask for His blessings when you have some time to ponder. You should use this little window of time to offer passionate duas to God in which you can express your entire being.

Just keep in mind that it doesn't have to be something you memorize; it can simply be something sincere you say from the bottom of your heart. So inhale deeply, close your eyes, and express your true feelings, and know that Allah SWT hears and answers every sincere dua.

The following duas can be read if you need some motivation:

1.

اللَّهمَّ أنتَ السَّلامُ ومنكَ السَّلامُ، تَباركتَ يا ذا الجلالِ والإكرامِ

As-salaamu alaykum, tabarakta ya dha al-jalali wal-ikram, in the name of Allah.

O Allah, You are the Source of Peace (As-Salam), and peace comes from You. The Majestic and Noble, you are blessed.

(According to the Islamic prophet)

2.

اللَّهُمَّ أَعِنِّي على ذِكْرِكَ، وشُكْرِكَ، وحُسْنِ عِبادَتِكَ

Allahumma a'ini 'ala thikrika, wa shukrika, and husni 'ibadatika

Help me, O Allah, to think of You, to thank You, and to worship You in the best way possible.

in Sunan Abi Daud

Three. Ayatul-kursi

ٱللَّهُ لَا إِلَٰهَ إِلَّا هُوَ ٱلْحَىُّ ٱلْقَيُّومُ ۚ لَا تَأْخُذُهُ سِنَةٌ وَلَا نَوْمٌ ۚ لَّهُ مَا فِى ٱلسَّمَٰوَٰتِ وَمَا فِى ٱلْأَرْضِ ۗ مَن ذَا ٱلَّذِى يَشْفَعُ عِندَهُ إِلَّا بِإِذْنِهِ ۚ يَعْلَمُ مَا بَيْنَ أَيْدِيهِمْ وَمَا خَلْفَهُمْ ۖ وَلَا يُحِيطُونَ بِشَىْءٍ مِّنْ عِلْمِهِ إِلَّا بِمَا شَاءَ ۚ وَسِعَ كُرْسِيُّهُ ٱلسَّمَٰوَٰتِ وَٱلْأَرْضَ ۖ وَلَا يَـُٔودُهُ حِفْظُهُمَا ۚ وَهُوَ ٱلْعَلِىُّ ٱلْعَظِيمُ

Al-Hayyul-Qayyum, in the name of Allah. It says, "Laa ta'khudhuhu sinatun wa laa nawm," and "Lahu maa fis-samawaati wa maafil-ard." Man zal-lazee 'indahu 'illa bi-iznihi. It's good to see you, bayna aydeehim and maa khalfahum, and laa yuheetoona bishay'im-min 'ilmihi illa bimaa shaa'a. Huwal-'Aliyyul-'Azeem wa Wasi'a kursiyyuhus-samawaati wal-ard, wa laa ya'uduhu hifzuhuma.

Allah! Only He, the Ever-Living, All-Sustaining, is a god (deserving of worship). He is not overcome by fatigue or sleep. Everything in the universe, including what is on earth, belongs to Him. Who could possible appeal to Him without His approval?

Only what He wills (to reveal) can anyone understand His knowledge, even though He fully knows what lies ahead of them and behind them, Only what He chooses to reveal can anybody understand His knowledge, though. The preservation of both the earth and the sky does not exhaust His Seat, which spans both. Because He is the Highest and Greatest.

Surah Al-Baqarah, 2 vs 255.

Read the English-translated Duas After Prayer.

Conclusion

We can communicate with Allah SWT through the lovely act of salat. It is a means of affirming our spiritual relationship with the Almighty and of expressing our love and submission to Him.

With all of our brokenness, we stand in solat before Allah (swt), pleading for His pity and forgiveness. We grovel before Him, confessing our frailties and requesting His direction. We fall to our knees in front of Him, acknowledging His greatness and pleading for His blessings.

Solat serves as a reminder of our ultimate goal and sense of meaning in life. We are made aware of the value of being thankful, patient, and persistent in our daily lives.

If we turn to Allah in humility and sincerity, He is always there for us. He is the Most Merciful and Forgiving, and He enjoys hearing from His servants. Efforts to construct solat would not be in vain, according to Allah s.w.t. He even makes a vow to support us as we carry it out:

وَأْمُرْ أَهْلَكَ بِالصَّلَوٰةِ وَاصْطَبِرْ عَلَيْهَا ۖ لَا نَسْـَٔلُكَ رِزْقًا ۖ نَّحْنُ نَرْزُقُكَ ۗ وَالْعَٰقِبَةُ لِلتَّقْوَىٰ

Encourage your followers to pray and to practice it religiously. You won't need to give anything to us. We take care of your needs. And only (the people of) righteousness will ultimately benefit.

(Al-Taha, 20:132)

May Allah guide us all to perform solat honestly and sincerely, and may He accept our prayers and reward us in this world and the next.

Reference

1.

http://prayerinislam.com

2.

http://raiyanfoundation.com

3.

http://www.muslimaid.org

4.

http://www.islamicfinder.org

5.

Shams-din Muhammad al-Khatib al-Sharbini, al-Iqna fi halli alfaz abi shuja, Dar al-Kutub al-Ilmiyyah, Beirut, Lebanon.